IN MY ARMS

Zac Porter

SEARING CLARITY

Cover image by Ally Merino.

searingclarity@gmail.com

ISBN: 979-8-9943903-0-6

Acknowledgements

Thank you to my friends Alex Weidman and Nick Paitsel for the time they spent with this manuscript and their willingness to talk it through with me. Much of my creative output would not be possible without their support.

I

Dad said that getting out in the woods would help us take our mind off things; Grandpap's viewing is at two-thirty. *Curiosity pulled me in slowly and first I observed the low water from the safety of the creek bank.*

Up at four-thirty in the morning.

Still dark. Downstairs: The flick of Dad's cigarette lighter.

Visualize him in the stillness: A hand running through thinning hair, sitting at the table in his undies. Elbows on the arm of the chair, looking at a point in the corner of the kitchen. Throw on my clothes: long-sleeved t-shirt and thick jeans. Over top of them a pair of insulated overalls. Walked downstairs with the overalls on, then decided against wearing them just yet. It would be too hot inside. Best to leave them by the door. Take them off carelessly, letting them crumple by the door.

As I imagined: Dad at the kitchen table; the lights are low. I turn them fully on and go in.

"Good morning," I say.

"Good morning," he says.

His belly hangs over his waist and he looks at that point. Hasn't turned the fan on and the room is stale with cigarette smoke. I don't make a move to turn it on because I don't want him to think the smoke bothers me because it doesn't. I breathe it in. Look at him: The bags under his eyes are deep purple and swollen. *It was the dog days and the water struggled to slip over sediment slip between rocks and move onward to the river. I know it's hard to think of water struggling but it did and I think in doing so it says something about this place and says something about us.* Did the man sleep? Something pulls at him from within.

Mom isn't home, she had gone over to her mother's, along with her brothers and sisters. They didn't want her alone. Should I be there with them, instead of here, with my Dad? Would he still have wanted to go hunting if it was his own Dad that — ? I look at him looking at that point in the kitchen. Why aren't we there? Was it that they didn't love each other enough to be there for each other? Did love have anything to do with it? *Sometimes water struggles.*

Or was it the uncontrollable direction of life itself, pulling two people further and further apart, toward their lonely destinies; two destinies that only intersected in a moment of passion.

Yet there were times that I was certain they loved each other. Made for each other even. Like when they'd listen to music together. And sing together. But they were stuck. *Sometimes water struggles.* Trapped in circumstances and trapped in situations outside their control. Can I say I even know them? Who are they and what are they like when I don't see them? I know I am different inside of this smoke-filled kitchen; by the creek; with my friends; different alone. What is Mom like—right now? Is she crying? She might be crying. If I try I can see her in my mind at Grandma's house crying. As far as I can tell, Dad isn't affected in the slightest.

Sometimes there were black snakes in the small pools of mountain water. Snakes are evil and I liked to shoot them with the pellet gun Dad had bought me and I liked shooting them because I don't think evil had a place in that water.

He hasn't taken his eyes off that point like there's something awful and invisible he's having a staring contest with. To be honest, I'm not really affected either. *How could I not think the creek doesn't cry mineral tears when it's filled with evil snakes coiling, eating, drinking, shitting, and laying eggs in its gentleness?* Grandpap was vague to me; I'd only seen him a handful of times and he never had much to say. Still, if I close my eyes and imagine Grandma's house I can feel the absence that's making Mom cry right now; he wasn't so much as vague as he was a presence; if I had went with her to that house then that absence would be all over me; I would not know it but it would make itself felt like it's making itself felt right now when I think of her; an impression; a pain that talks through nothing, through a point.

Dad grabs the paper. "Hand me the scissors, will you?"

I snort. Pull open a small drawer to the left of the oven. It's filled with junk and I fumble around for a minute until I feel them. Hand them to him and he starts to cut a clipping.

"What is it?" I ask.

"Grandpap's obituary," he says. "We'll laminate it for your Mom later on."

He cuts the clipping and sets it among a small pile of papers that had accumulated on his portion of the table.

"There's coffee if you want some."

I look in the cabinet for a mug. Pick out a red Fiestaware one; I like the heaviness. Pour the rest of the coffee in from the pot.

"Are you going to want some more?" Dad asks.

I think about it. "No," I say. Dad grunts.

"I'm going to want some more." He gets up and rinses the pot at the sink behind me. Doesn't look at me and stands there in his undies indecent. I sip my coffee. It's bitter and tastes like shit but I drink. Fills the water reservoir and tosses the old filter. New one in with four scoops of Maxwell House. Reaches into the cabinet and grabs his large worn silver Stanley thermos. He flicks the coffee machine to brew and the machine gurgles back to life with a thunderous roar that fills the kitchen.

"I'm going to get ready," Dad says. "When the coffee starts, take the keys and start the car."

He goes downstairs and the heaviness of his footfall on the stairs makes a steady thump that recedes into the basement.

After a few moments, the patter of coffee announced itself against the glass of the pot. I grab the keys and go to the back door, where Dad's tall rubber boots are neatly placed. I put them on and go outside; my feet swim in the big boots. *I shot them. Every time I saw one I shot it because they couldn't stay in the water forever. They had to come up for air and when they did that I sent them back down below.* Dawn is not here yet and the soft glow of kitchen light pushes into these last moments of darkness. It is cold, but not cold enough for a frost yet and I think it might just frost tonight and the dew shimmers in the electric glow. Walk down the sidewalk and unlatch the gate to get to the garage. There is a small yard to the side of it that Dad parked the car at at an angle. There is a perfectly good little driveway in front of the garage door. Why does Dad always do that? He's going to tear the yard up when he backs out. *When I'd shot them all after a month or so I started collecting beer cans and set those up in the creek and shot those.* I unlock the door and sit in the driver's seat. Pump the gas twice, put the key in the ignition, and turn it. The car cranks, the sharp grinding noise piercing night's perfect stillness and the engine roars. I rev it just a tiny bit and smile. Put the heat on full blast and then right back up to the house. Take Dad's boots off, put them back, and sit down at the table again. Dad is still downstairs. He left his cigarette burning in the ashtray. Now that I've been awake for a minute I see just how hazy it is in here. I hear those heavy footsteps.

"Here," Dad says. Tosses me a bright orange beanie. "It fit you?"

I try it on. Fit well enough, a little loose.

"Yeah," I say.

Dad sits back down at the table. "Smoke this one then we'll go."

My coffee was already getting cold but I keep drinking it anyway. *There were no snakes twenty-five yards up or down the creek and I started to get tired of beer cans and I didn't like to do beer bottles because then the glass shattered and made a mess and I didn't like the thought that if anyone walked through here they'd be sliced open and it'd be my fault.*

Dad stubs out his cigarette at about halfway. "All right."

We get up and I turn the light off as I leave the kitchen.

I put on my overalls, and then my boots. We have matching pairs, as we bought most things in sets for the two of us.

"Grab my satchel," he says. "I got the gun."

I grab the satchel and hold the back door for Dad. Flashes me a quick glance and he pulls out the keys to lock the door. *I moved to birds.* I let the glass door fall against its frame loudly; he sends me another, more menacing glance that tells me not to do that. Walk down. I get ahead of him to open the gate.

At the car, I toss the satchel in the back seat. He passes me the gun in its canvas case and I carefully lay it down.

"Be a second," Dad says. He goes into the garage and grabs a thick black garbage bag. I get in. Warm. He opens the driver door to pop the trunk. I look at him in the rearview mirror; he tears the bag down the side to make it a long, black plastic sheet. Lays it down in the trunk as a lining. He gets in. Puts the car in reverse and lets the gears do the work, careful not to tear up the yard.

"Why'd you park in the yard?" I ask.

"Let me do the thinking," he says.

I keep my mouth shut. *I don't know why I did but I did. Was just tired of beer cans I guess and they were the next obvious thing.*

He drives us down the alley. A left onto First Street and then a right onto Carolina Avenue. Then the exit to get on Thirty.

We don't say anything to each other.

"Remember when you start to drive," Dad says, "respect this hill. Always be in the right lane unless you have a good reason not to be."

I don't say anything. *At first my intentions were nothing, the kind of lightness that comes out of the fogginess of boredom, but the lightness of birds proved to be an unforeseen challenge and my intentions turned brutal.* Dad is in a hurry and speeds up the hill. He jerks the car toward the exit to get on Route Two, south towards

New Cumberland. He gets himself out a cigarette and lights it, cracking the window. This seemed to calm him down and he slouches back in the seat.

"Your Grandpap never cared for me," Dad says, after a while.

I often missed.

"Why?"

"When I got together with your Mom I tried calling her one time and he said, 'Ike don't you ever call this number again.' Click. Fucking hard-ass. Things changed after you were born though."

A tension sprouts. *I was left with the impression the birds sensed this impending dread the same as when you feel someone else is watching you. A set of eyes somewhere setting you on edge but you don't know the reason why you feel that way or why you're being watched. I don't know why I did but I did.*

"Did Mom like him?"

"I don't know. It's different for her, you understand. That's her Dad. Dad is always Dad."

Knowing that I was the cause of a sense of dread filled me with power.

Darkness fades—the world is prepared for its birth into another day. Yes, another day—the sun rising in the east; unseen at this moment; for us—only the first rays; caught and refracted by valleyair; rays that reveal the horizon foregrounded by the soft foothills; the dew in the grass more visible as the hue slackens from darkness into blue; a deep blueness crawling over the earth; the brief blueness of dawn; it is fall but despite its being fall there's a sense of everything plunging towards its winter bleakness; everything will be bathed in light.

The power of taking life.

Dad turns left, taking us into a holler. An old friend of his Dad's, Rich, lets him hunt on his property. A relationship that in my mind is veiled, belonging to a different era of life that only reveals itself in flashes, like here, and then only in the obscurity of a stranger's home. Rich's house is humble: Dark green siding with two levels, the lower nearly being a part of the hillside; there is a large porch overlooking the woods we were about to enter. Dad slows down, bringing the car to a halt in a grassy area before the tree line.

"Don't slam your door," Dad says, getting out.

I sat on the creekbank patiently and robins and sparrows came and went. I turn back to grab the satchel and gently open the door. Try to close it as softly as possible; close the door until it is about four inches from closing, then pop it shut. Glance at Dad. Was that too loud? He didn't look. Still has his door open. He's shoving his cigarette in a small gap in the driver's side mirror. The cigarette sticks out, burning. Opens the back door and grabs the gun. Unzips the case and takes it out—a Remington .308. Dad has owned the gun for as long as I can remember. The barrel is black steel; it has a black scope. Otherwise it's enveloped in lightly stained hardwood. A humble rifle if there ever was one. *A robin stays on a patch of uncovered grass a touch too long.*

"You're going to be firing it, so you're going to carry it," Dad says. He pulls back the rifle's bolt action to ensure it isn't loaded. Passes it to me. There is no sound but the sound of our breath.

We start on the trail. There is a small stream separating the property from the woods; I hold the rifle close to my chest and hop over, into the woods, following Dad. *I know it's hard to think of water struggling but it did and I think in doing so it says something about this place and says something about us.* The blue shades of night have changed, becoming lightness, revealing the woods, slowly, timelessly.

Fall: The leaves on the forest floor still bright with yellows and oranges, the occasional red; but many of the trees are dead, *I fired the pellet gun* structures that for one reason or another passed into another kind of life; soul-less; hollow; left with no defense to the Nature they are still part of; deformed by the presence of insects and termites, who take this opportunity to feed and everything in Nature has its place; and yet what about us; where are we; where am I; what is the relationship to this countryside that is a part of our lives; do I feel at home; do I feel like I can dissolve into something beautiful like bright yellow and hollowness; something that swallows me.

Its wings fluttered and it failed to fly. It tried. No. I feel little for the woods. *It tried again.* The woods evoke nothing; the leaves crushed under my boot say nothing; the presence of birds only sound; about hunting itself I ———. *After a brief struggle, the robin died on the patch of grass. I didn't immediately investigate. I sat looking at the creek, my heart thumping and on that dog day the sun beat down the heat like of a kind of judgement being passed.*

It is something that had to be done and so it was done in the same way were the woods a necessity; those hills are mute; those hills are not a container; not something that can make my life greater. *A kind of judgment I was just becoming acquainted with.*

After a while, Dad and I make it to the shack that he and his friend put in the woods years ago. It's a primitive set-up: About twenty feet tall and made of decaying scrap wood—a miracle that it still stands. *I shouldn't have done it. I shouldn't have.* The foundation is four wooden beams cemented into the forest floor. I look behind me. *I shouldn't.* Dad carried concrete all the way up here? Or his friend did? Perhaps they got a vehicle up here?

The shack itself is the four beams enclosed by plywood on all sides; the beams have additional support, with planks screwed into them, wrapping around the structure in random crisscrosses; they threw everything and the kitchen sink at the shack. For the final touches, they hung up camouflage netting that must have been purchased from the Army-Navy Surplus store in East Liverpool, along with screwing vegetation/brush onto the sides.

Dad labors up the ladder first. *It was a nasty, irresponsible thing to murder an innocent robin.* When he reaches the top, he tosses down a thin nylon rope that I tie the gun to so he can pull it up. I do a fisherman's knot around the metal component where the strap attaches to the wood, tug on the knot, and say, "Good to go." *Why then did it feel righteous, good even, to kill the snakes?* The rifle goes up and then I climb. I'm up in a few moments. Dad leaves two stools up here year-round; he wipes mine off with his hand and I sit down.

"Satchel," he says.

I unclip it from my waist and hand it to him. He takes out the .308 rounds and loads three into the rifle. Passes it back to me.

"Make sure the safety is on," he says.

The answer: snakes were a biblical evil and by killing them I did something that God himself did something in-line with an idea of punishment but the robin was different and as far as I could tell it never had a reason to be punished and a kind of shame of what I've done is in my thumping heart as real and as thorough as quiet water's gentle ebbing.

I look; the safety is a small clip on the left side of the rifle. If it is pushed forward, the gun won't fire, backwards, the gun is live. It is pushed forward.

"Safety's on," I say, leaning the gun in a corner of the shack.

Dad undoes the lid from his thermos and pours himself a cup of coffee into the lid.

"Want a sip?" Dad asks.

"Yeah."

Dad passes me the cup. *I looked to a pool of stagnant water the mosquitos made a home of and the flies were quickly aware of the new scent the fresh scent of blood and they dumbly made their way over to the tainted patch of grass and I laid the pellet gun down on the grass the barrel pointed away from the house like I was taught and the safety's on and the smell of its fresh oil doesn't give me the tinge of pride it did the night before I already decided I wouldn't oil it that night already decided that I'd let the water and air oxidize the barrel's alloy into the beginnings of rust joining the march of rust that's a part of everything here.*

The heat bleeds through the thin barrier and into my hands. Take a sip and pass it back to him.

"Thanks," I say.

Dad says nothing.

The shack overlooks the immediate brush in front of us and the hillside we had come up to get here; that hillside, to our left, is dense with trees, brush, and thorn thickets. To our right, the shack overlooks an opening between two hilltops; a small field with yellowing grasses that come up about waist high.

Dad looks over the field; I keep my eyes on the brush in front of us and to the left.

The act of scanning the woods quickly lulls me to sleep; I stare at some undefined point in the woods to look as if I were being diligent. In truth I put my best foot forward by listening; a deer passing through would crush sticks and leaves.

Still, I don't close my eyes. That would risk pissing Dad off, an anger that would boil in the woods since he wouldn't let me have it here.

Is it possible that he's barely keeping it together too? pretending too? I glance at him; his approach is serious; this is life or death for him; I watch his head move back and forth over the field, a hypnotic effect. How is he not putting himself to sleep? He had to be laying it on thick for me. If he were here alone he would be taking a nap right about now. That's what everyone does.

I went down the creek bank carefully taking steps on the moist but flat rocks until he reached the patch of sunscorched grass whose edges were shades of brown the only green down close to the dirt where that poor robin lies dead.

In front of his son things had to be different.

Dad reaches into his jacket pocket, pulls out a pinch of snuff, and tucks it into his lower lip. I sensed he was about to turn towards me; I pretend to look over the woods with the same seriousness as he does.

"I'm going to walk the back of the field and try and push something towards you," Dad whispers.

"All right," I say.

I scoot out of the way so he can get by. The shack sways slightly.

"Make sure you have the rifle ready," he says, and goes down.

I watch him walk through the woods. He goes up, through the brush, and then makes a right, disappearing. I close my eyes and listen; I hear the snapping of twigs underneath his heavy footfall.

Soon, that too, disappears.

I look to the field to my right.

Nothing.

I grab the gun. I pop the scopecap off the rifle and start to scan, from left to right. Nothing. Put the scopecap back on and lean the gun in the corner of the shack. Dad left his coffee. Take the Stanley, undo the cap, and pour myself a cup. I try to find the point I was staring at before but it's useless. I pick a different one. If I look at it long enough, I can enter a kind of trance, with the world slowly spinning around the point until I come to my senses. *I kneeled over it and a crow sitting in a tree ten yards up cawed, letting his brothers know danger was at hand. I looked into the robin's black eye. Where I hit it the feathers were ruffled.* But where was I looking? I look at the dense brush down to my left. Hear the scuttling of leaves. Too light for a deer. It is without doubt a bird or a chipmunk hopping about under cold October sky. What is Mom doing right now? Still early morning. Probably asleep. The only one that might be up is my uncle Jason. Standing in the kitchen drinking the first coffee of the day under this same sunlight. Were my cousins there? Gabe? Probably. Am I the only one not there then? The only one who had no good reason not to be there? I close my eyes and put my hands in my pockets. For a second I feel sleep tug at me. Probably good that I'm not in an atmosphere of imperturbable melancholy. Take a deep breath in. Let it fill my body till I'm swollen. Let it out. One by one, I crack my knuckles. Dad would be pissed to hear the sound. It'd scare the deer away, he'd say. I look around. What deer? I'd say. I pick up the rifle and pop off the scopecap and scan the field again. Spot Dad. He'd made it to the back of the field; I see his bright orange beanie, the exact same one as he gave me.

He is smoking a cigarette.

Doesn't that scare the deer away?

I follow him with the scope, in the middle of the crosshairs. *I shouldn't have.*

He's looking down at his feet.

I looked into the robin's black eye

He starts to walk along the back edge of the field; if there is a deer lying down, it will be pushed toward me.

I follow Dad along the back of the field in the scope. He glances up at me and his eyes widen. Makes a line right back to the shack.

I feel his weight climb back up; it sways.

When he sits back down he glares at me.

"Did you have the gun pointed at me?" he hisses.

I resolved to bury it; the only atonement that came to mind. I climbed up the creek and went in through the backdoor to get the keys to the toolshed.

"Ye-s," I say.

"Don't ever point a gun at someone."

"But we forgot the binoculars."

"I don't give a fuck. Use your eyes."

I am tense; the exchange puts my body in the grip of fear; a dark hand, passing over.

"You understand, don't you?" Dad says.

I don't say nothing.

"You don't ever point a gun at someone."

"All right."

"Say you understand. I need to hear you say it."

"I understand," I say. "Why don't we care as much about the deer?"

He doesn't answer; he smacks me upside the head.

We sit there. A tear streams down my face. I turn away and wipe it, so he doesn't see I am being a bitch. I remember we kill deer because we need meat and if we use this meat instead of buying it we'll have money for other things and that's the only kind of thinking allowed in this shack. *Grandma sits at the kitchen table spellbound by the television and doesn't notice. I went out and unlocked the shed; on the walls were garden rakes, pickaxes, pointed shovels, and square tipped shovels.*

There is a dense rustle in the brush in front of us.

"Rifle ready," Dad says.

I pick up the rifle, undo the scopecap, and slowly lean it on the banister. I don't look through the scope yet.

"There," I whisper, pointing at the deer.

"Where?" Dad says.

I point agitatedly down and in front of us.

I grabbed a square tipped shovel.

It is a button buck; its nose to the ground, nuzzling an unknown scent in the leaves. I don't have a clear shot; the deer is coming out of the brush and between two trees; I locate the deer in the scope and wait.

In the patch of grass I dug a hole two feet deep and two feet wide. I looked in the hole. I wanted it to be deeper so I dug down a little further. I carefully put the robin on the shovel with my foot and lowered it in the hole. The crows had stopped cawing when I left but now they've started again and in a moment of distraction and anxiety I looked to the tree upstream and saw three of them peering down at me. I ignored this and continued, looking at the robin in the hole. I sprinkled the dirt over the robin until the hole was filled.

There is a moment and I am called to it; necessity in cold October sunlight. I follow the deer with my rifle.

"Wait," Dad whispers.

I do.

A minute and a half passes, the deer nuzzling the same spot on the forest floor.

Is it picking up our scent?

The deer walks into the open.

"When you're ready," Dad says.

I flick the safety off and put the deer in the crosshairs. To the left of the shoulder, in the middle of the body. That should be close to the heart.

I take a deep breath and let it out.

Again.

Once more.

Once more.

On the third breath, I let the air slowly leave my body.

I pull the trigger; the gun erupts, slamming into my shoulder.

"Did I hit it?" I say.

"I think so," he says, smiling. Hurriedly, he packs his things.

Dad goes down the ladder first. When he is down, I tie the gun back to the rope. Lower it down. Clip the satchel around my waist and I go down too. The need to be quiet leaves me as if washed right out of my soul; we walk to the spot where I shot the deer, the leaves loud under our feet. From the shack, the deer was about twenty-five to thirty yards out. Dad lights a cigarette; the need for silence has lifted itself from his body as well as between us; he swings his arms freely and the seriousness of only minutes before has vanished, replaced by what I thought was a mood of giddiness.

We stand about where the deer was. Dad lowers his head, looking at the leaves, walking in small circles. I watch him.

"Don't just stand there," he says. "Look for blood."

I lower my eyes to the forest floor. There is nothing that suggests the presence of deer, let alone struggle, and it is impossible to distinguish anything. Still, I look.

"Over here," Dad says, crouching down.

He picks up a yellow oak leaf. Hands it to me.

There are two small specks of blood on it. How did he see that?

"Are there more leaves?" I ask.

"I found it right here," he says, indicating the place with his foot.

We walk, making a perimeter around the spot. There. I crouch down. Another blood-splattered leaf.

"Here," I say.

Dad comes over. "Nice," he says.

We repeat the process, only it becomes easier. Dad finds the next leaf, and then another, quickly, picking up a distinct and heavy trail of blood; the blood, dark red against the light brown leaves; dark against the pale yellow; dark against the hues of red and orange; wet against my boots.

We walk about another twenty-five yards up from where the deer was shot. The button-buck had fallen behind a log.

"There he is!" Dad says. He is smiling, looking back at me, the sun to his back, his figure brought into relief by the sunlight; his face worn by work in a steel mill, but in this moment—young, full of the small pride that fills a father when a son partakes in something he's done all his life; his eyes, the bags have receded slightly, the difficulty of early morning overcome by nothing other than life moving forward. The deer lies lifeless on the leaves.

A sadness passes, carried by October light, October wind, that was implacable, my shoulders fell.

What if my life was worth —— a moment of instinct?

I bowed my head in prayer. I'm sorry, I said.

The feeling is soon overgrown by dull excitement, the excitement of taking part in tradition; the excitement of my Dad's excitement; I had passed into something.

"Pass me the rifle," Dad says.

I do.

He takes the gun, approaching the deer. He points the barrel at its neck and pokes it; at first slowly, and then two more times in quick succession.

"Have to make sure it's dead," Dad says. "Don't want it running off on you and don't want it to suffer unnecessarily."

"He didn't make it very far," I say.

Turn around. Can still see the shack.

"No. Not far at all. It was a good shot."

We stand for a moment, looking at the deer.

"Pass me the satchel."

I unclip it from my waist, Dad unloads the rifle, letting the unused bullets fly out onto the ground; he leans the rifle against a tree and picks up the bullets. He takes the satchel from me and puts the bullets in a pocket. Gets his hunting knife and field dressing gloves.

"Hate this part," Dad says, placing the satchel next to the rifle on the ground.

"Glad I don't have to do it," I say.

"You will one day," he says.

I nod.

"Well," Dad says.

He kneels, opening the plastic gloves and putting them on; they go up to his elbows. He kneels, taking the knife out of its sheath and inspecting the blade.

"I need you to hold the legs open," he says.

I crouch down, glancing briefly at the deer's inert black eyes. *I looked into the robin's black eye*

I grab the right leg and hold it so the deer is spreading its legs, revealing the soft white belly. With the knife, Dad makes careful incisions, cutting through the hide, then a thin membrane so that the organs are exposed; I see the stomach; I see blood. *I didn't know exactly who I was praying to or what I was praying for; it was an abundance of feeling that the silence of prayer matched as if prayer were a shape in which to reign in all that is formless and the silence of the request and its mysterious answer in the guise of quiet water a soft judgement.*

Dad turns the knife around so that the skin is caught in the gut hook. Then, he rips up to the chest.

"Hold those legs close together," Dad says. "Don't want blood sloshing everywhere."

I do as he says. He takes out the bloody knife and sets it in the leaves beside him.

"All right let's turn him over," Dad says, grabbing the front legs.

We turn it over; the blood pours out; over the leaves; pooling; running downhill; the steam rises off it, into the air. We hold the deer stomach-down for a few moments and turn it back over. The blood is wet on the hide, staining it red.

"Let's pull it back a bit so I don't have to kneel in the blood."

Dad grabs the front legs and we move the deer a few feet. He resumes his work and I hold the legs back open to give him room. He works from the bottom-up. I turn my ahead away and look at the trees; somewhere a bird twitters. I feel Dad's tugging and pulling on the deer. He mutters to himself in frustration, putting the organs in a pile to his left. Steam comes off them.

"Dad, do we have to do anything with those?" I ask, nodding at the organs.

He glances up at me, with hardly a pause in his work. "No," he says. "There's other things out here that need to eat too."

He takes his knife and cuts something out from inside the deer. Holds it in his hands and looks at it for a moment; the lungs, in two dark red deflated bags, torn.

"You punctured the lungs," Dad says. He puts them out towards me, like an offering. I bend down and look at them more closely; there is a hole in one of them at least, where the .308 round brought the deer to death, or, at least just moments afterwards. I thought of what I knew about lungs. I'd only seen real ones once. For class they brought in pig's lungs to show us a demonstration of what a healthy set looked like. I felt a kinship then yet now the distance is unmistakable. I am alive. Dark blood spread over the lungs in a vain effort to stop death.

And then, nothing.

"You look like you're going to be sick," Dad says.

"No, I'm all right."

"Man up. You did this. Now you have to own it."

I nod. He puts the lungs with the rest of the pile and reaches back inside.

The heart.

It is little in Dad's hands. Undamaged and limp and soft-looking.

"Your first deer you have to eat a bite of the heart," Dad says.

"Eat it?" I say.

"It's the spirit of the animal."

He holds it and looks at me, watching.

"You're messing with me," I say.

"No," he says, holding it in his hand. "I did it."

"No you didn't."

"Yes I did."

We are at a stalemate. He looks at me for nearly a minute.

The yearning for forgiveness in my heart swallowed the lightning flash of cruelty that occurred not long ago as if cruelty belonged to a different part of my life and my praying over this robin a kind of summer heat cracking open something good and away from the senselessness I disavowed in prayer.

A long minute.

I wept for the bird, wiped my cheek, and climbed back up the creek bank.

"Just kidding," Dad says. Tosses the heart on the pile with the rest of the organs. "We got to get going," he says. "Get the rope out of the bag."

I do and pass it to him; it is a long length of thick rope, with a noose around the end. Dad feeds the rope through the loop so that the new hole, when the rope is drawn, will close. He nods to the deer's front legs. I grab them, bunching them so that the head and front limbs occupy a small space; Dad puts the loop over the legs and head, then pulls the length of rope to tighten it closed. Then hands me the rope.

"You're dragging," he says.

He always makes me do it. I take the rope, holding the length over my shoulder, and wait. Dad takes off the gloves, crumbles them, and stuffs them into the plastic they were packaged in. Stuffs that into the satchel and buckles it around his waist. Slings the rifle over his shoulder and starts on the trail. I follow. At first the deer is heavy, but when the inertia is overcome it moves along easily. Dad lights another cigarette, and I drag the deer down the hill in a trail of smoke behind him.

We reach the bottom. I drag the deer over the small stream; for a moment its body stops the water. Then over and across the grass. Dad turns around. Looks as if he were about to say something but changed his mind. He unlocks the car and pops the trunk. Opens the back door and carefully puts the gun back in its case. I drag the deer so it's lying next to the car. I look at the meadow fully covered by morning light; Rich's house before us, peaceful. On the other side of it is a road curling through this small valley, leading across the hillside; in my mind I see the white Methodist church not far up the road; small, a model of Protestant humility. The road goes to the left, from where we came, and I can hear the occasional car passing by from Route Eight.

"All right, come on," Dad says.

I bend down and pick up the front legs; he grabs the back; we pick the deer up, carefully maneuvering it in the spacious trunk of the car. I look at the deer, scrunched bloody and pathetic on top of the garbage bags. Dad closes the trunk with a pop; we get in. *I returned the shovel, locked the tool shed, and went inside the house. Grandma remained in front of the television, a cigarette stapled to her right hand. She was in a kind of stasis unaware how time was passing; I quietly slipped past her and returned to the room, my Mom's old room, putting the pellet gun in the closet. I've made the resolute decision to leave it alone, to let the weapon rust.* Dad turns the key and quickly turns the radio all the way down.

"We got to hear your hunting song," he says.

"Hunting song?"

"The first song that comes on the radio after a kill. It's your hunting song. What station you want?"

I think on it.

"102.5," I say.

Dad dials it in.

"You turn it up," he says.

I do. A bluesy piano lick, with its own refrain, a pause, followed by the chug of a guitar riff.

"'Locomotive Breath,'" Dad says. "Great song."

Dad puts the car in drive, up the driveway, and makes a left to get out on the road and a right onto Eight, heading towards the Thirty intersection, then towards Chester. He lights another cigarette and rolls down the window.

*

II

"When we get home can't fuck around," Dad says. "We need to get the deer hung up and then get ready."

"Okay," I say.

"Maybe we'll skin it too if we have time. Maybe tonight after everything we'll cut the meat up and part everything out."

"What would you rather do: Sit with your grandmother and mope around all evening or work deer?" He says it lightheartedly, meaning a kind of joke I don't laugh at.

"I don't know. Maybe she wants her family to sit with her," I say.

Dad doesn't say anything. Rips his cigarette and blows smoke out of the window.

"Maybe so," Dad says. "Do you want me to drop you off after the service?"

"I'll have to think about it."

We drive down Thirty hill and take the exit into Chester. In moments we are home; Dad pulls the car into the exact same spot as this morning, angled in a section of yard, except this time he backs it in so that the trunk is close to the door on the side of the garage.

"We have to be quick about this," Dad says. "I don't want anyone to see."

"Why?"

"We didn't tag the deer in."

He sucks in a breath. "We don't need some snitch with nothing better to do calling the DNR on us," he adds.

"Do you think someone would really do that?" I ask. "Why would they even care?"

"That's exactly what you should think, but you just can't trust these people. Nosy shitters."

"Why didn't we tag it?" I ask.

"The state already rapes us. It's none of their business if we get a deer."

I don't say anything.

We get out of the car.

"Come on," he says, "let's get this hung up."

He opens the side door to the garage. Inside, there are things everywhere. In the middle of the floor is a chop-saw, next to it a drill press that Dad bought from a yard sale; along the wall a workbench that Dad built himself; it too was covered in tools, the surface hardly to be seen; above it a peg board is attached, from which the few organized tools hang. *When I consider him in this context, the context of his past, everything that was so certain destabilizes* Along the back wall is a wood-burning stove connected to the chimney.

"Want me to get a fire started?" I ask.

"No," he says. "We'll come back out later, when it's cooled down. I think it's supposed to frost tonight. Maybe we'll take care of it late tonight. Or in the morning. We'll see."

Dad stands in front of the stove. Above him is the entrance to the attic, where a pulley system hangs down from the rafters that he had gotten from a yard sale in East Liverpool. Lowers down the "deer hanger" —an iron triangle attached at the top end to a chain; on the left and right sides are hooks, to puncture through the heels of the deer so it can hang upside down. He pulls the chain quickly and I hear the pulley chains rattling against each other and the hanger is on the ground.

"Come on," he says.

We go back to the car and Dad pops the trunk. There's the deer. Crumpled and broken and red with those little horns. He looks around; there is no one to be seen in the alleyway. He grabs the legs and I grab the head; we waddle into the garage carrying the deer. As soon as the deer is inside I shut the door and we set the deer down by the hanger. He takes each leg, puncturing it through the tendon above the back hoof on each leg. Then he raises it by pulling a chain; I stand and watch.

"Go ahead and grab that copper tub. Put it under the deer once I get it raised."

I go and he keeps working the chains, raising the deer. It raises slow like times barely moving at all, bogged down by chains that haven't been greased since I was born. I grab the copper tub, so dirty it's oxidized into green and then into black from the blood of countless deer; it is disgusting, but this is its sole purpose. I sit the tub down next to the deer and wait. When it is high enough, I softly grab the deer's head by the ear with one hand, sliding the tub underneath of it with my other. I look into its hollow body. Bare flesh and bare bone.

"All right, that's it for now," Dad says. "I'm going to have a smoke. You can go get ready if you want. I'll be right after you."

"Do you need anything else?" I ask.

"No. That's it."

I go to the house. On the back porch, I stand and look at Dad through a small window that peers into the garage. He sits there, smoking, looking into the gutted deer. What is he thinking? Is that calming for him? In the kitchen, I strip down to my underwear and socks and throw my hunting clothes down the basement steps. I run upstairs, sprinting to see how fast I could possibly go. Three seconds. At the top I catch my breath for a minute and go into my room. Poke through the closet, pretending I have lots of clothes but the fantasy dissolves; I have one suit that my parents bought me two years ago for a wedding. A black suit-jacket and pants with a white undershirt and black tie that's appropriate for all occasions. I take it out of the closet and inspect it and make sure it is clean. The pants and the jacket look good enough, a little bit of lint on them but that's all. The undershirt has a little yellowing around the neck, from my sweat, but no one is going to see that. I lay everything out and go to the bathroom. Take off my underwear and socks and toss them in a corner behind the door where they'll live for a few days at least until the pile's so big the door won't open all the way. I look at myself in the mirror. My face: The eyes have little purple bags under them like that thing that was pulling at Dad; has been inherited; now passed on to me as my body approaches manhood; there are hairs on my chest from doing the things Dad said would put hair on my chest; I'm by no means skinny I eat good everyday not fat either but a touch husky like some part of childhood is clutching to something or clutching to the gentleness of my body. I'm not all hardness yet——I turn the water on so that it is unbearably hot and bring it back a little from there.

When I'm done I go back to my room and start to get dressed. My shoes are in the closet; I have the same pair as Dad—Deer Stags. They are cheap, made with fake leather that is peeling off the scuffs on the shoe. I lay them out in front of the bed. Put on my white undershirt, my pants, grab my shoes, my suit jacket and go downstairs. Dad still isn't inside yet. I go to the living room and turn on the television, sitting in front of it, to mindlessly watch until it is time to go.

*

We leave the house to head to Grandma's in New Cumberland. Out the back yard again.

Dad in his suite, me in mine.

Like two brothers.

Twins.

And yet I know this is impossible. A father and son cannot be brothers; fathers and sons have their place and so often in this place the feelings are intensified, brought to their highest expression where love and hate disappear into a point like what I think of when I think of him could be jaggedmountain that casts shadow.

Grandma's house is surrounded by cars; the driveway is full, we park directly in front of the house, on the sidewalk so to be out of the way. Mom is from a big family. She has three brothers and a sister, each with their own families. We walk through the door. Nearly everyone is grabbing their things, packing up to head to the funeral home. Carter's.

Mom is by the door.

"Hi James," she says to me. We hug and she gives me a kiss on the cheek.

"Hi honey," she says to Dad. They give each other a peck on the lips.

"You two look handsome," she says, smiling. I can see that the smile is forced, pushing back what must have been the somber mood of the house.

Grandma comes waddling in from the kitchen. She is frail and small but still filled with strength. Mom looks nothing like her except for a few mannerisms she's inherited. They share an affability, but physically, she mostly took after Grandpap, namely, in that she is tall.

It was hard to imagine Grandpap as a child; for me he was perpetually old. Even the images I'd seen of him as a young man and as a child had the quality of remoteness; it was unthinkable that he could've felt the things I feel; that he felt the pain of love. When he was my age he might not have met Grandma yet—was it possible the image of another woman filled him to the brim with excitement? That the warmth that spread through his body at those thoughts had nothing to do with what's become our family? That he lay awake thinking just hoping to catch a glance and a smirk?

When I entertain these questions; they approach a critical mass.

The question marks of what never was are weighed down with absurdity and the scaffolding collapses.

"There he is," Grandma says to me.

"Hi Grandma," I say.

"It means the world to me that you're here."

I give her a hug. Feel her spine through her clothes, in my arms.

What I do know of Grandpap's childhood I know secondhand; he rarely spoke of it. He went to a small school near Seneca Rocks—I know this because of a photograph of him with his class. There were five of them, including him, and he looked happy, careless.

"We were just getting ready to leave," Mom says.

"You can ride with us if you want," Dad says.

"Okay," she says. "Mom who do you want to ride with?"

"I'll ride with Elijah," she says.

I see my uncle Jason and his son, my cousin Gabe. I briefly waive. Mom, Dad, and I are back in front of the house. I go for the back seat.

"No you sit up front," she says.

"All right."

I sit shotgun and Mom is in the back. Dad turns the key and the car rumbles to life. We sit there for a moment, idling, while Dad waits for everyone to get into their cars.

"What's that smell?" Mom says, after a minute.

"What smell?" Dad says.

"I don't know," she says. She sniffs the seat. "It's faint."

Dad gets out a cigarette, prompting Mom to do so as well. They crack the windows and smoke.

"We went hunting this morning," Dad says, eventually.

"And?" Mom says.

"Yeah, we put it in the back."

"You had to go and do this today," she says, looking out the window.

Dad doesn't say anything.

"Fuck you Ike," she says.

Dad doesn't so much as glance up from the wheel. Takes it on the chin and blows smoke out of his mouth calmly.

Mom crosses her legs and drops the cigarette out of the window. "Fucker," she mutters. "You would throw a deer in the trunk like a fucking hillbilly," she says.

They are silent in the car and it's an intense silence that has a way of stretching out the moments; I try not to look at either of them.

It is a short drive to the funeral home, and we are in the parking lot.

Carter's Funeral Home in New Cumberland: A house from another era; the era of the industrialists; the roof supported by creamcolored brackets; the windows accented with creamcolored frames and hoods; four small pillars surrounding the small front porch but this life it had has disappeared. Now it belongs to us and belongs to death and all the rituals that death demands from us.

We pull along the side, waiting for the others. They are right behind us and the parking lot fills. I open my door and get out, standing in the lot, watching my family. My parents get out too. Mom's family are all plump people whom it is best not to irritate lest they flick the back of your head with their sausage fingers. Elijah, Crystal, Jeremy, and Jason. Jason is the closest in age to Mom and the only one I've gotten to know. Jason can play the piano; Jason a deep bellowing laugh; Jason full of jokes; Jason completely bald; Jason blue-eyed whereas the others are brown-eyed.

We stand; none of us dare go in before Grandma arrives.

Uncle Jason took Gabe and I down to Seneca Rocks. We stayed with Grandpap's brother, Uncle Bill. It was just to be a weekend trip. We left Friday. Gabe and I went to the same high school, so I packed a gym bag and after school I rode the bus home with him and we left when Jason got off work.

Men and women smoke in silence and I stand by. Nod to Gabe. He wears a boxy black suit and struggled to neatly tie his tie, the same as me. I don't want to talk to Gabe; he has a fat face like a bulldog's and I keep my distance.

Cloudless blue October day.

Finally, Grandma arrives with Elijah.

In Seneca the sky was dreary, a blanket of dull steel rolling on indefinitely, trapping us in the mood of winter. Bill came into a valley where there were a few buildings: A gas station, a post office, and from the looks of it a bar. Pulled in front of the gas station and left it running. Be right back, he said. Jason, need anything?

Pack of smokes if you don't mind, he said.

What kind?

Marlborough's.

Bill nodded and went in. Just the three of us in the truck.

You boys having fun? Jason said.

Yeah, I said.

Where is it that Grandpa is from down here? Gabe said.

Uncle Bill's house, Jason said.

Really?

They were raised in that house and when my grandparents passed, your great grandparents, that house was passed on to Bill, Jason said.

Oh, Gabe said.

What?

I don't know. Nothing.

Bill exited the gas station with another man; they were laughing. The man slapped Bill on the back and went to his own truck. Bill got in.

A friend? Jason asked.

Drinking buddy.

Passed Jason his smokes then out of the parking lot and down the road.

After a little while, the rocks came into view.

The family gathers around her and each of us take turns embracing her. She weeps.

"Oh, oh, oh. Da-ddy," she says. "I miss Da-ddy."

Her emotion creates a field that washes through us. Faces are grave. Dad's face hasn't changed since the car. He is a stone; he hugs her. Then Mom hugs her.

"I want to be with him so bad. O-oh," Grandma says, taking out her handkerchief.

Mom holds on to Grandma another moment longer. "He's in a better place," she says.

My turn.

"Oh sweetheart," she says, putting her arms out.

"I love you Grandma," I say.

"I love you too honey."

She weeps. "Oh, o-oh, o-oh."

I feel a wave of emotion and shove it down, a swell of water hitting a concrete wall. As suddenly as the feeling rises it disappears to somewhere unknown and ancient and formless.

The October sky is merciless.

Grandma recovers and then is onto Gabe. She goes in through the side door first and I take the opportunity to shake the hands of my uncles. Callused hands with fingers as thick as quarters. Perpetually dirty. Even now they haven't managed to get them completely clean of oil and grime. They purposely crush my slender hand but I refuse to let the pain register on my face. I'll learn to be a stone too. Jason sticks his hand out for me. Pulls me in harshly.

"Dylan! You son of bitch," he says, in a harsh whisper.

I glance to make sure Grandma's in. She's in.

"What's the matter," I say, "CIA got you pushing too many pencils?"

We lock hands and stare into each other's eyes. I want to laugh and at first it's hard but it comes out. I giggle. He squeezes my hand so hard I feel the knuckles smush against one another and I finally wince. Puts his hand out in front of him and makes a fist as if to check his nails. Smirks at me to show that I was nothing. I stop smiling.

"Hit the weightroom," he says.

I don't say anything. Jason is an ogre compared to me. I bow my head and solemnly follow him inside.

The rocks themselves are an exposed crag made of Tuscarora, overlooking the town below. The crag a light gray bordering onto white; brilliant against the contrast of bare trees and snow, mostly bare, as if the trees gave up on that section of the mountain but there were a few that dared to find their way along the steep cliff. The upper ridges were jagged, with a significant notch near the middle where muted winter clouds rolled through.

Grandma is speaking with the director. He and his brother run the funeral home. The Carter brother speaking with Grandma is short and sweaty with pale skin and bags under his eyes. Curly gray hair that looks sewn into the scalp. Everyone knows he is a boozer and has an awful raspy cough that announces itself with stubborn frequency. His suit hangs on his body as if his arms and shoulders are made of broomsticks. Younger Carter isn't much better off. Whenever either one of them looks at me I avert my eyes. My uncle Elijah wants to speak with the younger Carter and pulls him off to the side. He places his paw on younger Carter's shoulder and hands him a cassette. The Platters. One of Grandpap's favorites.

The coffin is in the back center of the viewing room, flanked by flowers on both sides. Light slants fall softly through two windows, making the room warm. Some flowers were sent by distant family, some arranged by Grandma herself, some sent by Grandpap's friends. There is a large bouquet on behalf of the New Cumberland Nazarene Church. Grandpap wasn't exactly devout but was amongst the dedicated and that counted for something.

One by one my family inspects the coffin.

There it is, Bill said. Isn't she something?

Yeah, I said.

Next to me, Gabe fumbled with a small bag and pulled out a camera. Took it out, wound it, and I heard the click of the shutter. Jason took out a cigarette and rolled down the window.

Even though we were approaching the Rocks, I had the feeling they were remote; an alien heart; something so far from my understanding, yet right there, coming closer and closer. It was hard to think this belonged to me, in the sense that I am from here.

I am from this very mountain.

But it has nothing to do with me.

The mountain was silent, indifferent to everything below

I stand off near the entrance and watch. My family's eyes flicker around the room. Glance at everything other than the obvious. In the presence of death we are unsure of what to say or do.

"Hey James," Gabe says.

"Hi Gabe," I say.

He stands there next to me letting the adults get closer to the coffin.

"Can't believe Papap is gone," he says. "He just looks like he's sleeping. Could wake up any second."

"He looks peaceful," I say.

Gabe nods and joins his dad; I join my own group, standing behind Mom and Dad.

My older cousins arrive. They are a preceding generation and I don't know them and they don't know me. Young men and women. Some acknowledge me with a head nod, others not at all. They match the uniform of my aunts and uncles. Dark suits and dark dresses. Some with a pale flower pinned to their dresses.

The family mingles with the new disturbance. Avoiding the inevitable. Dad talks with Mom's brothers. Mom stands by herself. I gravitate towards my cousins but I am silent. I feel alone.

Dad moves to me. Places a hand on my shoulder. "Let's see him before the others get here," he says.

I nod and follow. Black lacquer surface that I see my reflection in; on the coffin my image a formless specter; untethered for a moment; I look away; come back to myself. Brass gilding around the edges: The handles for my uncles to carry the coffin when it's time. Dad stands in front of it; I'm behind him.

A mountain is just a mountain, after all.

What about the people who took this in day after day?

Were they like me, filled with a sense of the unforgiving?

A sense of the earth's brutal-ness?

Grandpap: A handsome man with a sharp chin. Freshly shaved for his funeral. Dressed in a light blue suit with a matching tie—out of place with its brightness implying a kind of hope; the color of big sky; a pale yellow flower pinned to the lapel; a small thin nose; eyebrows bushy and gray; he looks both frail and vital; his hair slicked back in the style of the "greatest generation"; his eyes are closed, a searching gaze fallen in unfathomable blueness.

Did the roughness of the feature make a deep impression on the minds of those who saw it? It was making an impression on me. A shadow claiming its spot in the light of consciousness; the outer trickling its way in. Yes—this feature was a kind of mood, a kind of presence, a kind of shadow lingering in the minds of everyone here— how did this distort feeling? Thought? Did the mountain make the warmness of feeling itself into its jaggedness? A place with no narrow ledges to hold fast to?

There are pictures in the coffin, displayed along the back inner edge. One is a picture of Grandma and Grandpap when they are young. His arm around her waist, on a picnic. I look. I know I'm indebted to the photo. There's a sense of distance, that the past is in this coffin is unable to be brought closer, an alien heart beating in my body.

What does it mean to be an embodiment of the past? a representation of family? to live within the family myth that has replicated itself like a germ finding bodies? What we call *generations.*

There are other photos. One standing in front of a beloved car; one with some of my uncles; one with the older cousins; one with me on my birthday; one of him alone, smiling with a beer at the kitchen table.

Grandpap's hands are crossed at the waist. Dad closes his eyes. Places his hands on Grandpap's hands. This lasts three seconds, that private farewell. Dad kisses him on the forehead and walks off to the left. I step up to the coffin, trying to conjure profound words to say to Grandpap's spirit, which I am certain hasn't left yet. I say, "Grandpap I love you. I hope you are in Heaven if it exists." More sentences and thoughts begin to form but none of them ripen, the beginnings of language vanquished to the emptiness from which they arose. I feel the presence of another behind me. I put my hand on Grandpap's, copying Dad. His skin no longer feels like skin but something inert and cold; the impression etches itself on me. I can't bring myself to kiss Grandpap. Kiss something inert and cold; I bow my head and turn away. Head over to Dad.

"Want to come outside with me while I smoke?" he says.

"Yeah."

Dad is familiar with the halls. Navigates them with ease. His own family has held funerals here since he was a child as well. We go out and the cool air enlivens us. Dad takes out a cigarette and smokes it in a way that presents his anxiousness. He looks to the hills, for comfort I think. Somewhere below is the river.

"I was never close with my dad," Dad says.

We don't look at one another.

I look at the hills. Blurs of yellow. Orangeness with a smattering of red; ecstatic; a profusion of color capable of sustaining meaning; how do you articulate meaning except in this kind of ecstasy——. The ecstasy of color.

"I used to hate my dad," Dad says.

"Why?"

"He used to hit us."

"You hit me before."

"I know," he says.

"Was it different?"

"I hated doing it."

He pauses for a second. He says, "I remember this one time I lost a sock in the gym at school and when I took my shoe off and there was no sock on my right foot he just beat the hell out of me."

I'm looking at the houses behind the funeral home part not knowing how to comfort my Dad and part not wanting to.

"With the belt," Dad adds. "Sometimes with the switch...you don't hate me, do you?"

"No."

"If you ever wanted to talk to me you feel you could do that can't you?"

"Ye-s."

"You're my best friend."

"You're one of my best friends," I say.

"Remember you don't have any friends," Dad says. "Your family is who is going to be there for you. Remember that."

"Okay."

Dad flicks his cigarette into the parking lot. "Better go back in," he says, making for the door. I follow and grab a handful of peppermints out of a bowl near the entrance, filling a pocket. Take one out of the plastic and put it in my mouth. Back to the viewing room. It's grown more crowded. Mom is in a chair near the wall in the second row. Take a seat beside her. She puts her hand on my shoulder but doesn't say anything. Is she feeling sorry? I look at the wallpaper. Ugly beige with dingy flowers. My uncles take their seats and Dad sits beside me.

People start to come in I don't recognize. Then Bill comes in. He goes to the coffin and shakes his head in disbelief. Comes over to us. "Ike," he says. They shake hands.

"Bill," Dad says.

"Don't give your old man any gray hairs," Bill says.

"I think I've already done that."

"I always liked this boy," Bill says to Dad.

Bill flashes a brief smile and then is off.

Variants of this interaction happened over and over with Mom and Dad. I could see in these moments that they were still treated like children; taken out of their adulthood; I see a secret part of them; or—their something secret returned and left me unscathed as someone who didn't belong to that set of memories. Someone not quite an adult yet. They were forced to return to the invisible game of respect that stretches between generations. Yes, the voyage into adulthood is kept a lonely secret—that is certain. Is it because there is nothing to say about the journey? The loneliness: That, despite your upbringing; despite who everyone thinks you are; despite the culture of this valley—you are a wild heart, fallible to gentle winds; there is nothing that can determine us with absolute certainty; our destinies have the quality of disappearing.

We pushed on up the mountain; it started to snow. A light, dry snow that only made itself felt when the occasional flake touched my face. We walked single file and there was no one else out; Bill was first, I was second, Gabe was third, and Jason fourth. The forest became denser, and I lost track of where we were, hypnotized by the falling of footsteps and the monotony of tree cover.

All of the chairs are full. A man I determine to be the pastor stands in front of a small metal podium. I figure he is the pastor from a particular countenance: An apologetic gesture in the lines of his face matched with graveness. He wears a black and white suit like the rest of the men.

Clears his throat. "Good afternoon," he says. "For those that don't know me my name is Pastor Steve. I'm the pastor at the New Cumberland Church of the Nazarene. We're here today to celebrate the life of Larry Nolan, taken from us too soon but we know that, despite our sadness, this is a part of His plan for each and every one of us."

"Yes," I hear in the back.

"We know," he continues, "that Larry is with the Host of Hosts and we bless His name."

"Amen."

Pastor Steve clasps his hands in front of his chest. "I'd like to lead us in prayer," he says.

I glance around. Everyone bows their heads and I do the same, but I keep my eyes slightly open, looking at my shoes.

"Heavenly Father. We know you have just given the keys over to Larry at his new Heavenly home where family and friends of days past are joyously celebrating his arrival. He is home. We know that Larry accepted you into his heart. We remember what you said Lord, 'I am the Way, the Truth, and the Life: No man cometh into the father but by me.'"

The clouds swirled and the sky darkened; the sun set would be around four o'clock and we were losing daylight. The snow thickened. Fat flakes fell heavily, covering the ground. About thirty to forty feet in front of us, was an overlook built by the parks service, but it was inaccessible, with yellow tape around it.

Come on, Bill said. Let's take a look at it.

We followed Bill right up to the overlook. He took the tape off and stood on it; the boards creaked and he hopped up and down on it to test how it would hold weight.

All right Jimmy, Bill said. Come over here.

Hold on, let me see it, Jason said.

Jason got on the overlook and did the same as Bill, testing the platform. Then walked off it. Bill sent him a suspicious glance.

All right James, Jason said. Go ahead.

Bill and Jason walked off; I walked on.

I looked to the little town below, barely visible in the falling snow here the world was completely open

this feeling of openness gently captured me sealing me into itself in an illusory solitude

I took a deep breath in and the breath that filled my body I imagined to be different than all the others I'd every breathed it was the breath *of the mountain peak——mountainbreath I wanted*

to fill my body to the brim with I closed my eyes and felt the flakes cover me is this what dying is like a kind of letting go a mountainbreath where I let the world swallow me and I become a kind of nothingness a quietude like the dry leaves I'd crushed under my foot

buried under delicate snow

I stepped off and Gabe came up to the overlook. I watched him, to see if he was experiencing what I experienced what I'd felt emerge from deep inside me softly.

Gabe looked and smiled down on the valley.

Ahead of us, the ridge climbed further, becoming the crag.

Pastor Steve prattles on. What do the Apostles, or Moses and Aaron for that matter, have to do with me? with this Ohio River Valley? Already riverwater and valleymountains have etched themselves onto me. Pastor Steve concludes and welcomes the elder Carter brother to the front of the room.

"Okay," he says. "We'll do our final visitations. We ask that the friends of the family come first."

He nods to a corner of the room. "Twilight Time" by The Platters plays.

A line is formed leading to the casket between the two seating areas. Men and women, some I know and some I don't dab their eyes.

Something hard cracks in me and my eyes are wet. I wipe them with the tops of my hands. Mom reaches into her purse and hands me a tissue.

"I'm fine," I whisper.

"You just hold onto it," she says.

Crumple it and put it in my pocket with the peppermints.

The emotion passes. Brief. A spark. A flame. Down into the depths of October. I am hardened. A rock.

Somewhere between child and man.

It is the family's turn to say goodbye. Family in the back of the room join the line. One by one they approach the black coffin and say a goodbye. See: Rough hands on the interior of the coffin. See: Secret messages. Prayers.

Finally, it is my turn to get in line. I stand behind Mom and Dad. They place a hand on the coffin and exit left. I look at Grandpap one last time. He looks the same as before.

I lay my hand on the white silk. I have no thoughts and emptiness pervades my body; not emptiness; an awareness of everything; my Grandpap, my Mom lightly sobbing, my cousins behind me—I had merged with the world; not mute not dumb a presence. I lean forward and kiss Grandpap's cold forehead, lowering my head, going out with my parents.

There is a purple flag on top of the hood of the car. White print on it that says: CARTER'S. Mom and I climb in. I sit shotgun again; she rolls her window down and lights a cigarette, tilting her head, blowing smoke out of the opening. The front door of the funeral home opens. Her brothers—the pall bearers—carry the coffin to the back of the hearse under the direction of the Carter brothers. They move carefully and awkwardly, as if carrying a human diamond. Dad stands outside and watches. When it is done, he gets in and starts the car; he cracks his window and mimics Mom, lighting a cigarette and blowing out the smoke. The hearse pulls out and we enter the procession. I look in the windows of my family's vehicles: More titled heads, all blowing smoke. Some wiping eyes.

We turn right onto Route Two. On the left: The outline of Dad's face against the Ohio River. We turn right to head up the backside of Rolling Acres Road. The openness of expansive Ohio Valley contrasts with the up-close fall foliage; its sense of small grandeur; the intuitive perception of the world undergoing change; that we were a part of it; moving through it; no, up close there is the pervading sense of decay; the crumbled leaves; color draining from them; the warmer pulses folding into grayness. Grandpap's skin still on my lips is doing the same—this ecstasy of life.

We pull into the cemetery. The hearse pulls in front of the chapel. Dad cuts the engine and meets Mom's brothers by it. Younger Carter opens the back door and they carry the coffin inside the chapel.

The chapel is small. Not enough room for everyone. I make myself small and squeeze along the back, near the door.

The pastor is the last to arrive. He leads us through prayer, wishing the soul of Grandpap well on its journey to Heaven, and wishing that his soul continue to watch over his surviving family members. With that, Pastor Steve reads a verse and we quietly exit the chapel. I rejoin my parents and we walk to the burial site.

It's grown cold and I think that Dad was right it might just frost but I'm sweating, sweating a cold sweat.

A hole was pre-dug where Grandpap would be laid to rest. His tombstone is black, in the shape of a heart with an angel cradling it. On it is his name and the month and year of his birth and of his death in white detailing. Grandma's name is on the other side, but just her birth month and year are engraved. There is a kind of simple machine hovering over the hole.

The pall bearers load the coffin into the hearse; it drives to the burial site; then they unload him for a final time. The Carter brothers direct them on how to place the coffin onto the machine's rack; the sound of hands on coffin and the rustling of straps.

We stand.

Stillness.

In the surrounding woods birds chirp, oblivious.

Everything is how it should have been.

Pastor Steve opens his Bible and reads us another verse.

When we got to Bill's truck, there was a slight feeling of panic. The snow was really coming down and showed no signs of letting up. Even Jason appeared perturbed.

Can you handle this? he said to Bill.

Bill laughed at him to suggest he had been handling it every single day before Jason was even a thought. Gabe and I each had about an inch of snow stuck to us. Brushed each other's backs off and got in. Bill cranked the truck. Cranked for about seven seconds and finally turned over.

She has trouble starting in the cold from time to time, he said.

He started us back along the same route we had come by, except in the opposite direction. Bill went to put his windshield wipers on, but they weren't able to keep up with the wet snow and kept sticking to the glass. Gabe and I glanced at each other. Bill cursed under his breath. Rolled down the window and stuck his head out.

That's better, he said.

Moments passed. Was he going to drive the whole way home with his head out the window?

He was.

Jason, Bill said. Light me a cigarette and hand it to me.

He did, and Jason laughed while Bill's hand fumbled for it, and the feeling spread to us.

I laughed and Gabe laughed as well and I see
Bill full of mountainbreath
full of mountain
and I knew a man could always return to
this—
become dust and become jaggedness and
daunting
that way, living beyond

Pastor Steve nods to the Carters who then announce that the service is concluded.

The mood brightens a little—only enough for people to begin chatting with one another and say goodbye.

I walk with my parents back to the car. Two men I hadn't noticed walk up the hill, to the burial site, presumably to lower the coffin and cover the hole.

To begin their lonesome work.

*

III

Dad and I are going to the store.

"Going to the store"

It's in winter in Appalachia; cold; gray; the sky itself like congealed blood; reflecting the slow river, spotted with chunks of ice.

"Going to the store"

Why is it that I'm here for this? He never asks me to go to the store.

We never go to the store.

Mom goes to the store.

She is sick today. A fever.

Are we getting her medicine?

I am young and this time is distant; an awful echo; yet alive; lonesome.

We get in the car.

There is something different about Dad. It's the way he holds himself today.

He carries anxiety. His hands—they grip the steering wheel tightly.

We go out of town. Towards East Liverpool. Across the yellow bridge.

Dad takes the opportunity to grab himself and me a beer. This is my first. It's cold in the garage and we stand looking at the dead deer.

Mom comes out and stands at the edge of the door. She's cold too and has changed out of her funeral clothes into a sweater and jeans. She walks closer to us and looks at the deer.

"Were you nervous?" she says.

"A little," I say.

"It looks like you did a good job," she says.

"Your first deer," Dad says. He hands me a Milwaukee's Best and Mom gives a suspicious look Dad immediately brushes off. "You've earned a beer today," he says.

I take the beer indifferently and crack it open like my entire life has been a kind of training for this moment. I sip it and my face scrunches up at its bitterness and Dad laughs.

"Now this don't mean you can just be drinking beer whenever you want now. You understand?" Dad says.

"Yeah."

"It's a special occasion. You can drink as much beer as you like when you're of age. All right, let's get working on this thing. James go ahead and get a fire started."

I shake the ashes out of the stove and take out the tray full of ashes holding my face away from it and dump them in a tin trash can outside whose sole purpose it is to hold the ashes. I slide the tray back into the bottom of the stove and go to the house to grab old newspapers. Last Sunday's paper should be plenty.

I sit them beside the stove and chop some kindling wood using a small hatchet that Dad and I refurbished about a year ago. We found it at a yard sale and worked the rust off the blade and put a new edge on it along with a handle that I sanded and varnished myself. Honed the edge using a fine chisel, just sharp enough to make easy work of the planks. I put the newspaper in the stove first and build a small cone around the crumpled paper. Go to the workbench and grab a can of oil, squirting a little on the structure and I push in a bar on the outside of the stove that closes off airflow to the chimney. I grab a match, strike it, and put it to the newspaper watching the fire a moment as the yellow tongues catch until the first sound of firetouched wood cracks and I'm sure that it will take.

I look down. Fields of ice dance softly across the surface of the water.

We are in Ohio.

I know that to my right it will take us to Midland, the home of steel mills and music.

Left will take us to Calcutta, Beaver Local, and Rogers.

We go left.

Dad, where are we going?

Going to the store.

Need to make a stop 'fore we go that way.

We get off of the highway. To downtown East Liverpool.

I'm happy to spend the time with Dad.

He'll work twelves for almost a month. If they are midnights, then no one sees him. He goes out and comes back in mid-morning.

Then straight to bed, wordlessly.

He's been on midnights.

I grab a log from a bin and the splitting maul and cut the large log into quarters. Do it for three logs.

The sound of crackling kindling is loud enough; I pull back the bar and allow airflow to the chimney. Open the stove and put the three logs I chopped inside. I'll wait to turn the blower on; the fire isn't hot enough. It'd just blow out cold air. Dad leaves and it's just me and Mom. She stands there and smokes. Glance in the copper tub and I see its wet from the little bit of blood that must've dripped in there since we've been away. When he's back it's with a collection of knives, mostly small and nimble to more easily work the flesh of the deer.

"Hold the legs," Dad says.

I stand on the backside holding the iron bar above my head so it doesn't move while Dad starts. He cuts through the hide on the inside of each back leg. He works his way under it to feel the membrane between hide and muscle. He cuts a full circle just below the final joint of the leg and works his other incision to this higher one. He's done this for what seems like forever; like it's his nature; the hide is fully separated from the muscle and my hands are getting cold on the steel and I think maybe I should just go ahead and turn the blower on. Dad takes the exposed hide and rips down with force, throwing the deer from my hold. Work the hide off from the ankle down. The hide on one leg is just hanging off the deer like an unfilled jacket sleeve.

"Sorry," I say. Dad keeps working the knife between the hide and flesh, ripping down the hide on the other leg. Works the hide off the backside until he reaches the tail.

I'm happy but his mood is making me question my happiness; like two feelings, held independently, can occupy only so much space.

He grips the wheel. My happiness is snuffed out.

I'm thinking of the river, how it must be old; older than it's possible to think.

We go past the Giant Eagle.

It's on the left of the car.

I've never been this way before.

We've passed the store.

Why has Dad taken me with him?

Am I supposed to help him with something?

He always likes it when I help; I think he needs me.

There is a house halfway up the hill.

Dad grabs a pair of bolt cutters and clips off the tail. The sound sends a shiver through my body as if one of my own pinkies were cut off. Dad is expert and surgical. He tosses the tail into a trash bag and continues working the hide off in total concentration. Before long he has it worked halfway down the deer.

"All right, come here," Dad says. "Stick your fingers in there on that side and I'll get my side. We'll rip'er down."

I go for it and stick both hands underneath the hide. I can feel the ribs of the deer on the backside of my fingers. All right. Pull. Dad and I yank down on the hide. It budges about two inches. Pull. We yank. Pull. We yank. Pull. We work the hide until it's down to the neck.

"All right."

Dad comes up for air and with his bloody hands lights a cigarette. "Take a break," he says. "Check on the fire."

I go and flick the blower on with my bloody hands and look at my untouched beer and ignore it and throw some more wood on the fire. I look again at my beer. I'll dump it out and pretend to have drank it when the moment's right. Dad's back is turned. I grab the beer and step outside, dumping it out behind the garage.

If he asks I'll tell him I had to take a leak because that's what we do sometimes just piss right on the side of the garage rather than go up to the house. Go back in. Dad is standing next to the deer holding a hatchet and a hacksaw.

"Grab those bolt-cutters," he says. I do. "Clip off those front legs," Dad says. "Below the joint. Don't want to waste any meat."

Dad parks the car.

Stay here, he says.

I don't say anything.

He turns the key off and the warmth ceases.

It's winter in Appalachia: cold; gray; the sky itself like congealed blood; my reflection in the window shield; small; feint; a ghost that exists in reflections.

I sit there.

For minutes.

I don't count them; I feel them.

I'm wearing an old military jacket. I zip it up and do the collar to protect my neck.

More than minutes.

The silence of a parked car has a shade of death.

Death, an open space, quiet country, unknown winter.

I look at the door of the house. It's rectangular with four smaller rectangles inlaid in each of the quadrants; it's dark brown and worn; but it is closed. Dad left his cigarettes. Should I smoke one?

I grab the pack and open it; there are many cigarettes and one is flipped upside down. I flip it back over and close the pack; I don't want one.

Where is he?

I take the bolt cutter to the deer's front leg. It's harder than I expected. It goes through the hide and the flesh but the bone won't give and I crouch holding the cutters near my center pushing in on the handles with all of my force and I hear the crunching of bone and the limb is amputated with the left side of the deer hide and dangling foreleg lying dumbly half-in and half-out of the copper tub. I do the same with the other leg and the struggle isn't as great this time now that I got an idea of how hard bone is. All that's left is the head. I hold the deer by the fleshy legs and the iron bar and Dad starts cutting through the neck with the hacksaw. The sound is awfulness the grinding of bone and metal and I turn my head away involuntarily. Dad struggles.

"Jesus Ike," Mom says.

"Son of a bitch drank his milk," he says. He makes a little headway and switches to the hatchet. Dad holds the button buck by the head and its little horns and tries to hack through. Bone splinters off the deer into the copper tub onto the floor and onto my leg. Halfway. He switches back to the hacksaw and he's through it: The head and hide have collapsed into this pathetic tub in a mixture of blood, fur, bone, and oxidized copper where the meaning of death has escaped us both becoming something low and mundane death a job hardly different than cleaning out the carburetor on a lawnmower a job full of frustration messes trial-and-error and the satisfaction of progressing towards some object but the mess of it all empties out the sacredness associated with life pulling it down into the filth and warmth of this garage into something intelligible on this October night. We take a break.

"When you get a minute go inside and get the steel containers," Dad says. "We'll start taking the meat off here soon."

I go out.

A brief flurry starts to fall, a gust, and snowflakes swirl

How easy it would be to be like those birds darting across the street;

they chase each other; how easy it would be to be like that

the snow falls the flurry brief

now something more; more than minutes a squall

I come back in with the tubs and Dad takes a hose and rinses out the deer. He's replaced the tub with a set of buckets ready to be changed out and emptied when one is full. I set the small steel bins on the workbench and make a makeshift table out of two sawhorses and a piece of plywood. I lay the stainless-steel containers out in a perfectly straight line. Dad lays out his knives on the table, feeling the edge of each to gauge its sharpness. He selects a Buck knife and lifts up his shirt and shaves the coarse black hair off his belly. In a moment there's a bald spot about the size of a quarter. "That's sharp," he says and nods with satisfaction. Mom shakes her head. She makes for the fridge and grabs a beer. Dad puts his shirt back down and starts to work the deer. He takes large chunks of flesh off of the back legs, putting them in the containers, works chunks of meat off the leg until the bone is visible. There are light brown hairs stuck to the meat.

Dad works the back-straps. Takes the knife and makes an incision parallel to the spine and about three inches from it on each side. Then takes the knife and runs it against the spine on each side. He cuts the ends one near the hind legs and the other just before the front shoulder. With the perimeter of the straps cut out, Dad sets his knife on the table and works each strap off the ribs with his hands: His fingers under flesh grating against bone he pulls down and away; at first they don't give but the membrane linking the two fails and the strip of flesh peels off. "This is the deer version of filet mignon," Dad says. He uses his knife to cut away stubborn flesh not coming off the ribs. He sets the knife on the table and shows me the strip. Holds it like it's a big fish and I nod and he gives it to me and I hold the strip of thick flesh in my hand and put it in the container while he works the other off.

When he's done he sits with his back to the fire and lights a cigarette, indifferent to the chunks of flesh underneath his fingernail.

"Go ahead," Dad says. "Get whatever meat off it you can."

I nod and grab the knife off the table. I like the Buck knife Dad used but not just for its sharpness but the bone handle contours well to my hand. I get small chunks off of the front legs and clean up any spots Dad missed on the back legs. Dad throws a log on the fire and aside from this the only sound in the garage is this knife working the deer and the stove blowing hot air.

Before long, the deer is skeletal; a night image.

"What are we going to do with the rest?" I ask.

"Dump it somewhere," he says.

"Is that all right? Shouldn't we do something with it?"

"What would you do?"

"I don't know."

"All right then we'll dump it."

"All right."

"Put the meat in the basement fridge. We'll grind it tomorrow. I'll cook us some back-strap tonight."

I get up to grab the tubs. I can only carry two, but I didn't account for being unable to open the door. Dad gets it for me.

The night air closes me in its silence; a different texture than the quietude of the garage; closer to emptiness that shatters the illusion that working the deer intricately created; hours have passed.

There's a noise from the house; how easy it would be, to be a crow, in this Appalachian winter with my only worry being that of the sky; what it will or won't do no father, no mother, only the same country as I've always known; winter; cold; gray; the sky itself holds countless mysteries inside its congealed blood; ancient; withholding something that I don't understand but that the crows embody in their simplicity; how easy it would be; all I need; no minutes; just openness; unlimited presence; the only shadows are the ones that lean in the afternoon; how easy it would to be more than words; more than minutes; more than feeling just the simplicity of being what I am; a son; how easy it should be; to be a son; how easy it never is; riddled with the shadows of complexity, meaning, the guesswork of feeling; of understanding feelings; what's expected of me; all unspoken; more than minutes; they don't understand; sitting in the silence of a parked car shows how loyal of a son I am; in this quiet country; am I supposed to be helping with something? I've never been this way before; but I was born on it; how easy it is; the path of a son in

unknown country that is mine and outside of me;
Mom is sick today; are we getting her medicine;
what is it that he's doing; need to make a stop 'fore
we go that way; I am young and this time is
distant; an echo; alive; I'm getting cold in the car
and I shove my hands deep into my pockets but I
don't know if it's working; the heat is gone and
snow is starting to settle on the windshield; fields
of ice collect small on the surface of the glass
erasing my ghostly image

I set the meat on the porch and prop open the door for myself. I take the trays one at a time and to the basement. I return to the garage for the rest of the meat: Dad hardly acknowledges me he's looking at a point somewhere on the garage door like he looked at that point in the kitchen this morning inside a different kind of emptiness where he's lost himself but my presence brings him back if only for a moment and he's looking back at the floor. I take the rest of the meat to the basement fridge. When I finish I grab a stool and sit with my back to the fire too.

"Okay you ready?" Dad says.

"Yeah."

Dad gets up and grabs a roll of heavy-duty trash bags and a set of thick rubber gloves. Unrolls three bags and lays them on the table. "Take one and hold it open," Dad says. I do and Dad puts on the gloves and picks up the bloody and wet hide and puts it in the first trash bag. I tie off the top and set it to the side. He takes the bolt cutters and uses them to snap off the back legs of the deer so they fit in the bag. Dad doesn't struggle and the force he applies is enough to go through the bone in a single movement. I hold open the bag and Dad puts in the two front legs. He moves the copper tub off to the side and lowers the deer skeleton onto the concrete floor. Undoes the back legs from the iron hooks and takes the bolt cutter to them as well. Limb by limb. The spine and ribcage sit naked. He grabs the hacksaw and starts sawing the deer in the middle of its body; the sound is no longer grating and grotesque. It has fallen away from those delicate sensibilities and joined the chorus of the everyday; something we perform because it is so; a part of an invisible set of rules that I've now taken into myself; forming me; an entire movement of this Northern Panhandle distilling itself and breaking apart like bone on steel.

The bagged deer is in the back of the car and we drive all the way out to New Cumberland, to Hardin's Run Road, a "country road" that follows the aforementioned run deeper into the hills.

This car reminds me of a coffin and the snow covering it likens to dirt falling over a grave and past the houses I can barely see the beginnings of a tiny forest; as of yet untouched; I look at the door of that house, rectangular, inlaid with four small rectangular quadrants, like all doors, symmetrical, beckoning; I'm cold and I can't stand how cold I am; I unlock my door and get out, heading towards the tan house that Dad went inside of; it is a short walk and it is a long walk; the crows leave their station on the wretched branch, flying off towards West Virginia I'd like to think how easy it would be; to go home——

There is only starlight and the faint glimmer of the occasional family home; the headlights can only do so much and Dad strains to see the road. The hills push in on us and on the car but the thin hum of the radio gives the impression we're separate from this landscape; passive beings cruising through the night with a job to do and not another care not a care for the trees drooping low over this road some branches reaching across almost and some vines as low as to glance the car around a sharp bend but still we are in this moment oblivious to Nature.

Mom is sick and she needs us, needs us now; I put my hand on the brass knob and twist; it is unlocked and I push it open; in this living room there is nothing; no couch; no televisions; no pictures; there are two lawn chairs, split by a small outdoor glass table; on top of it there is an ashtray filled with cigarettes and a folded piece of aluminum foil next to it; Dad, I call; there are no noises and I think he must be upstairs; I walk into the kitchen; the counter is littered with coffee cups; the sink filled with dishes; it stinks; there is a small table, against the wall; it has papers and papers on it, on top of the papers are two plates that have fresh bread; I glance at it and then I don't; I turn around; between the kitchen and the living room is a set of stairs; I start up them; more than minutes; at the base there is a small stained glass windows in the shape of a star;

We reach a part of the road where there are no houses in sight and Dad pulls off on the side of the road.

"Grab a bag."

We each grab one and I follow Dad as he walks into the forest. We don't go very far and are stumbling in the woods but when Dad decides it's far enough

*I look out it and I can see the snow has stopped
and everything is still and I hear the call of birds;
they haven't left for the almost heaven yet*

I don't count them I feel them

these stairs don't creak and that bothers me

*the silence of a closed space, telegraphing a
kind of life*

*I'm unfamiliar with, that of something
other than a son; I think about calling for Dad,
but I don't*

*nervousness has gripped my heart I'm not
used to the feeling; it controls my entire body, my
legs; I feel them twitch as I move up the stairs; I
hear a low noise*

*three bedrooms; two doors are open; there is
one that is cracked and I tip-toe to it, putting my
eye to the slit*

*on the bed are two bodies; what am I doing
here; she is younger than him by some years; she
lays on the bed on her back, with her head resting
against the wall; He is next to her; there is a bottle*

on the floor that he takes a swig of and there is

music; Under my Thumb, by the Rolling Stones

we stop and open the bags and the smell of deer carcass hits us point blank and we turn our heads but persist dumping the limbs and the body and the hide all into one messy pile

He lightly touches her face

after a moment she comes to

comes to life

she holds his face

they start to kiss; at first gentle

then it becomes more

that will sink into the earth like blood and the bones will sink into the earth to become decayed breaking down into its elementary particles only to be taken back up as organic matter as life. What these hills have seen. What's left of the flesh will be picked over by the vultures and we go back through the woods, to the car, into the night.

how easy it looks; I stand there; they grab each other

I stand there, watching; she moans softly and he says something

there's something incompatible about the sounds

about the bodies; for seconds, I sit there; where is he?

I back away

away from that room

quietly going out the door returning to the car

returning to winter

*

IV

Some time has passed and it is night. There's something terrible about the falling wind that shakes my window. I look out and I see there's no moon or if there is moonlight it's smothered by cloudcover. The television drones on and I lay there. I look out and see there's a small light, coming from the garage, coming out of ———. It drones and I lay there; I close my eyes hoping to slip into the arms of ———.

I do.

I don't.

*

Time passes. Momentless moments of sleeplessness. I've had enough; I throw on a pair of long johns and a shirt and go.

Soft footfall on hard steps. Mom is on the sofa; she is watching channel 9. It looks like tomorrow this cold front will be lifted. She looks peaceful in the artificial light; it must be soothing to her.

I leave it on and turn the volume down; she adjusts, aware something has changed. I go to the back door. The garage light is still on; I grab a jacket off a hook, put on boots, and quietly go out. Sleepless falling wind and I cross my arms and walk.

The door is cracked and a clean slant of garagelight falls on cold concrete. I put my face to the slit. Dad is there. The table is full of beer bottles and his eyes are open and he's leaning back against the stove (isn't it hot?) chin touching his chest.

He's not looking at me. He's looking down. At that point he looks at, wide awake, in

conversation with that —— communing with
it in silence.

*